How to Draw Stampy

Cat & The Gang

Blockhead Drawing Guide ft. StampyLongNose & More

Garland Group

Disclaimer

Table of Contents

Chapter 1 – Stampy Cat

Step 1

The first thing you should do is create the shape of this cat's nose and then add a long stem for the nose.

Step 2

Then, draw out the puffy lower part of
the cat's face while making sure his
chin is hairy, but not too hairy.

Step 3

Draw out the head and the face shape while drawing in the skinny pointed ears.

Step 4

Complete the shape of Stampy's ears in this stage.

Step 5

All you must do is draw in some rather thick eyebrows.

Step 6

Draw in the rest of his eyes, which need to be bright and big. Draw some slits in for the pupils and add a smirk for his smile. Erase any mistakes that you may have created up until this point.

Step 7

Stampy's face is now done. You can color him in if you would like.

Chapter 2 – Villager

Step 1

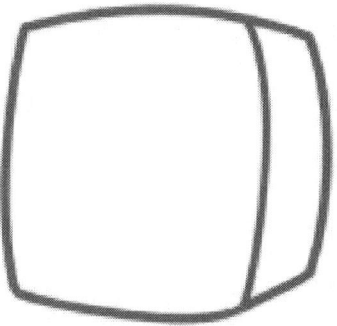

Create a rounded block shape for his
head while adding in the dimensional
look for this box.

Step 2

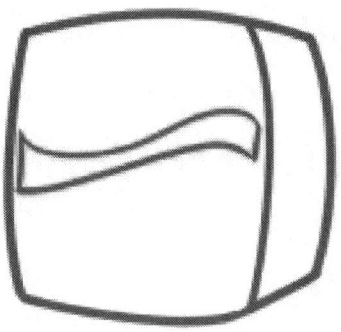

Next, add in the unibrow for the villager so you can draw a thick wavy line across his forehead.

Step 3

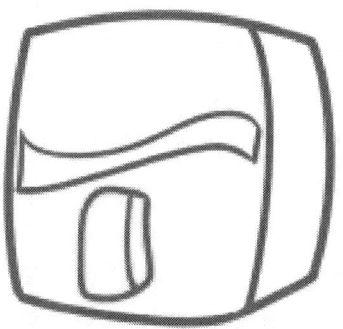

Draw in a nose in a long and block-like style.

Step 4

Draw in the box-like shape of the eyes.
Once the eyes are done, you can draw
in a frown for the mouth while adding
a frowning line at the corner of his
mouth.

Step 5

Now, we'll work on the body by
drawing in the torso and the arms. The
arms will be crossed one over the other
just as you can see over here.

Step 6

Add some details to his shirt and also his arm.

Step 7

Draw a whole shape for his legs in this step.

Step 8

Now add in the shirt lines with the
dimensional line going down the side
of his leg.

Step 9

Create a split to give the villager two legs and also finish up the detailing on the shirt.

Step 10

Draw in his shoes and erase any mistakes that you might have made.

Chapter 3 – Sky
Amy

Step 1

Draw the basic body for Sky. Draw it as accurately as possible to the sketch above.

Step 2

Sketch the blockhead for the creature while creating some sharp edges towards the corners of his head.

Step 3

Use some light and swift strokes to sketch out the hair that will cover his face.

Step 4

Sketch the glasses while adding some basic facial features to your creature.

Step 5

Start sketching the arms of your
creature.

Step 6

Now you're going to need to add a ton of details towards the inner body.

Step 7

Finally, start sketching in the legs that should also be very blocky. Congratulations, you're don with your drawing after this step!

Chapter 4 – Wolf

Step 1

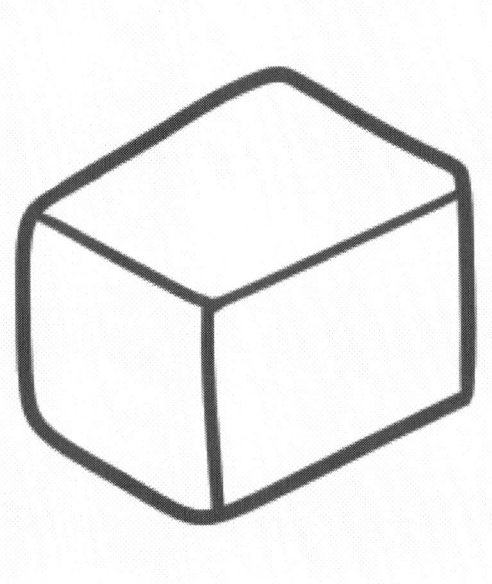

Start by making a basic outline and shape for your wolf. This will give it a 3D look.

Step 2

Using shape you made, start drawing
the basic outline and structure of your
head, face and snout.

Step 3

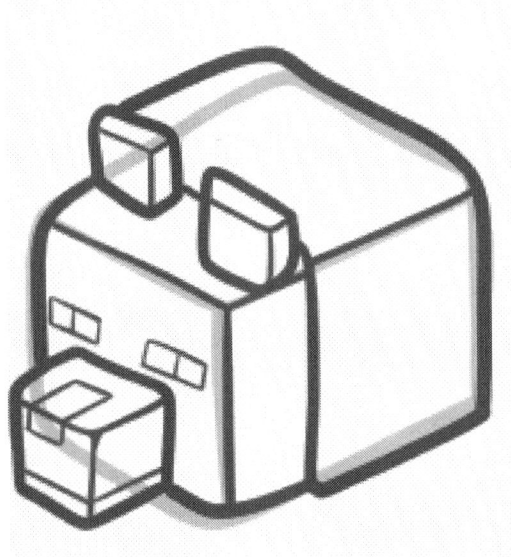

You'll now draw in the details for the
face while adding in the eyes.

Step 4

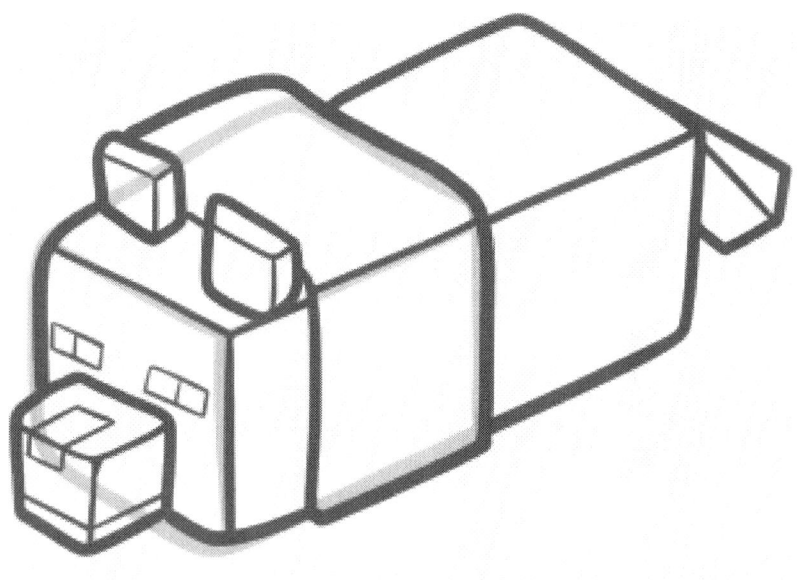

Now you're going to add a rectangular
body with a tail to your wolf.

Step 5

Add in the final details, which are the legs for your wolf. Congratulations, you're drawing is now complete!

Chapter 5 – Chicken

Step 1

Make an oblong box shape for the head.

Step 2

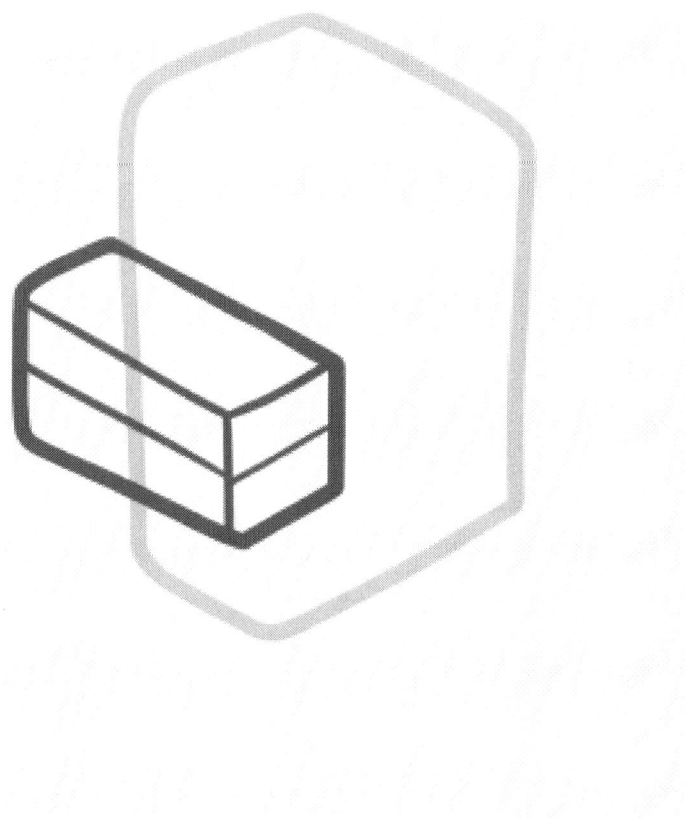

You'll now draw the shape of your beak for the chicken.

Step 3

Outline the shape you just draw in the first step while rounding off of the edges.

Step 4

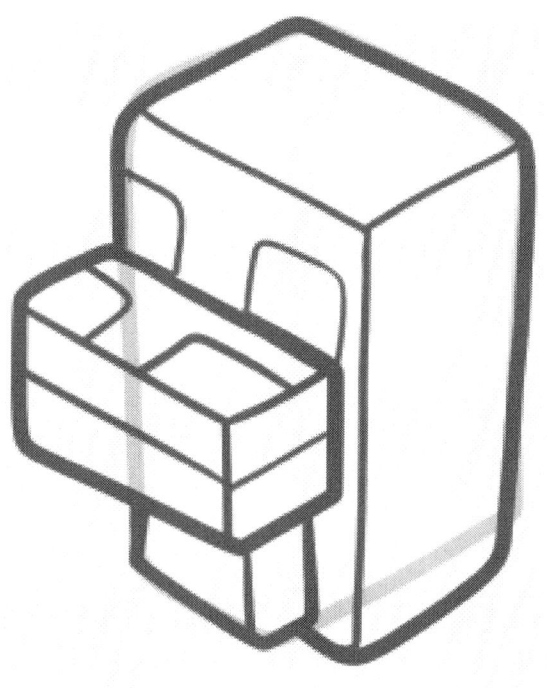

Add in the eyes while drawing some lines to shape out your head so it looks 3D.

Step 5

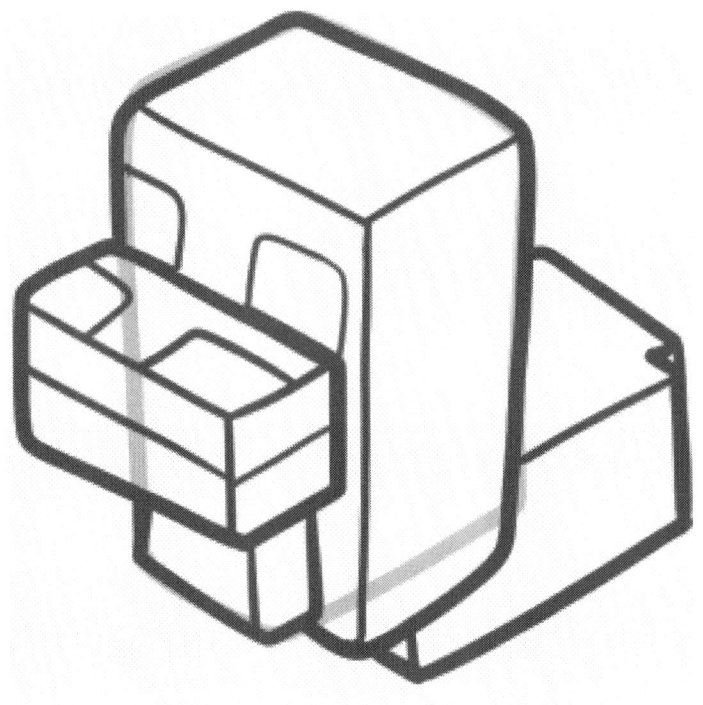

Draw out the body, which looks like a flat box.

Step 6

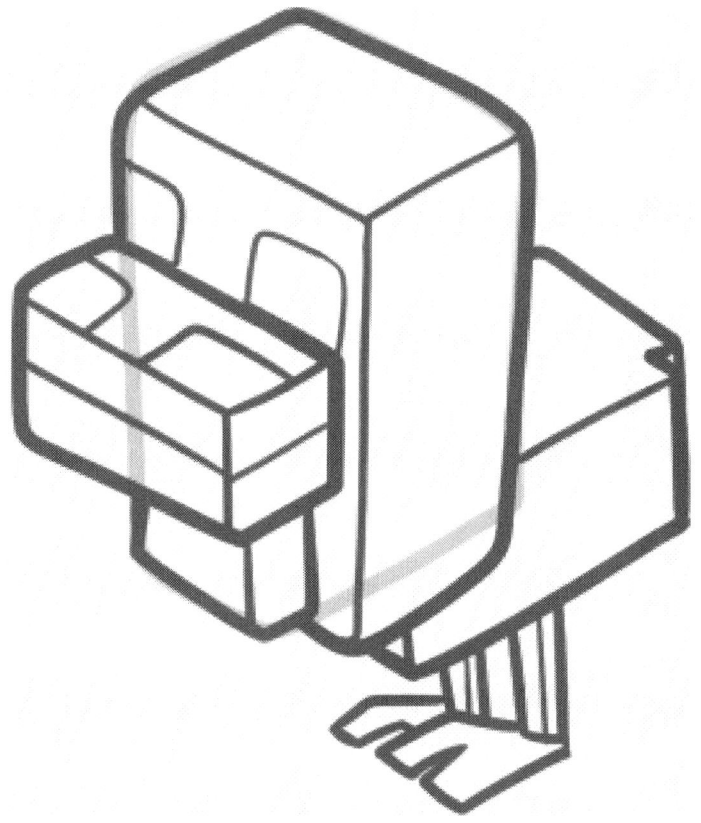

Draw out the legs of the body as well
as the feet for your chicken.
Congratulations, your drawing is now
complete!

Chapter 6 – Cow

Step 1

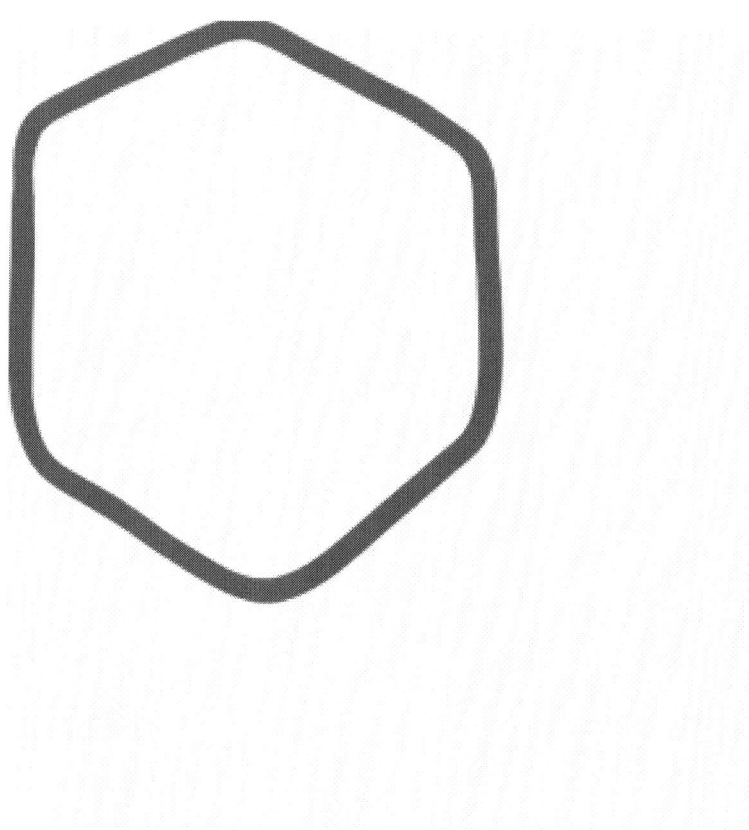

Create an octagon shape that will be a
square for the head of the cow.

Step 2

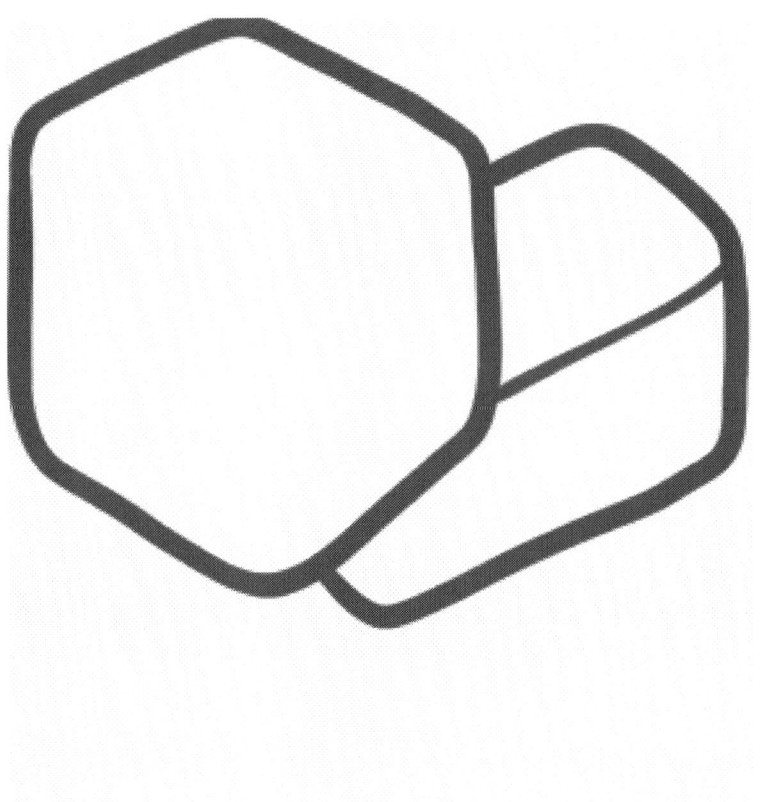

Draw in the shape of the body for your cow. It's almost the shape of a 3D rectangle.

Step 3

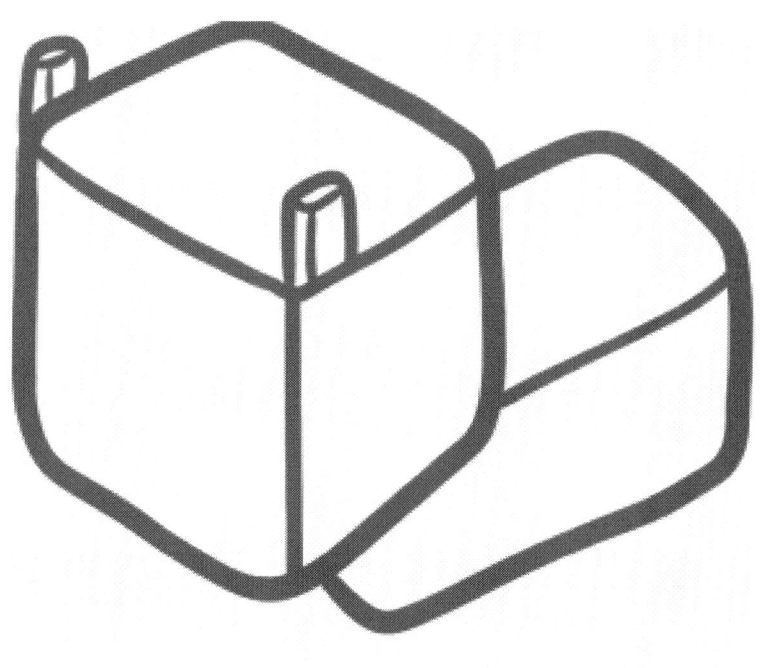

Create a box-like shape for the head of
your cow while adding in the ears.

Step 4

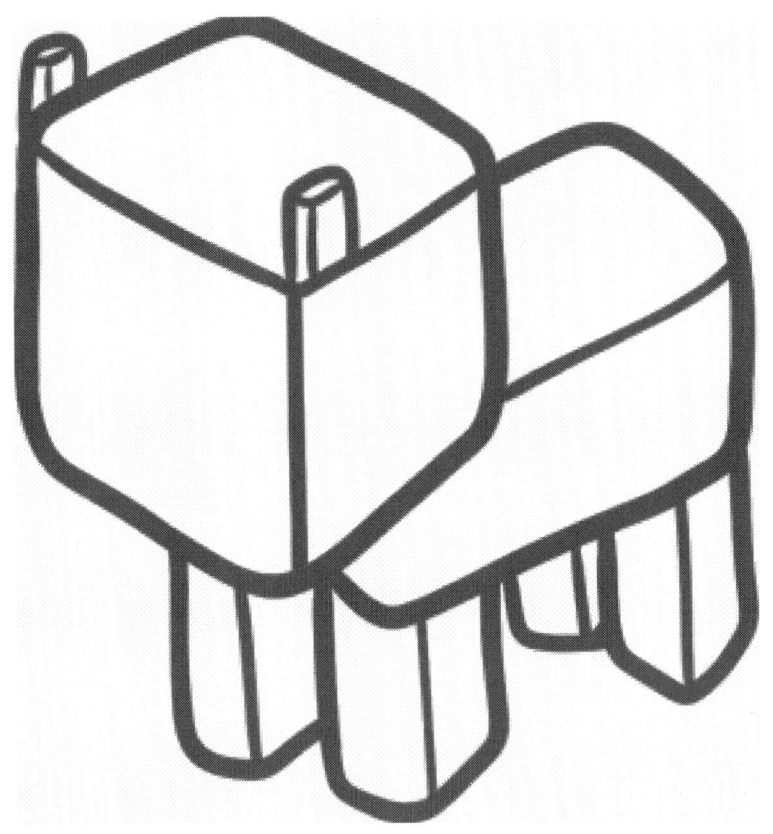

At the bottoms, add in the legs for your
cow. They will be nice long blocks.

Step 5

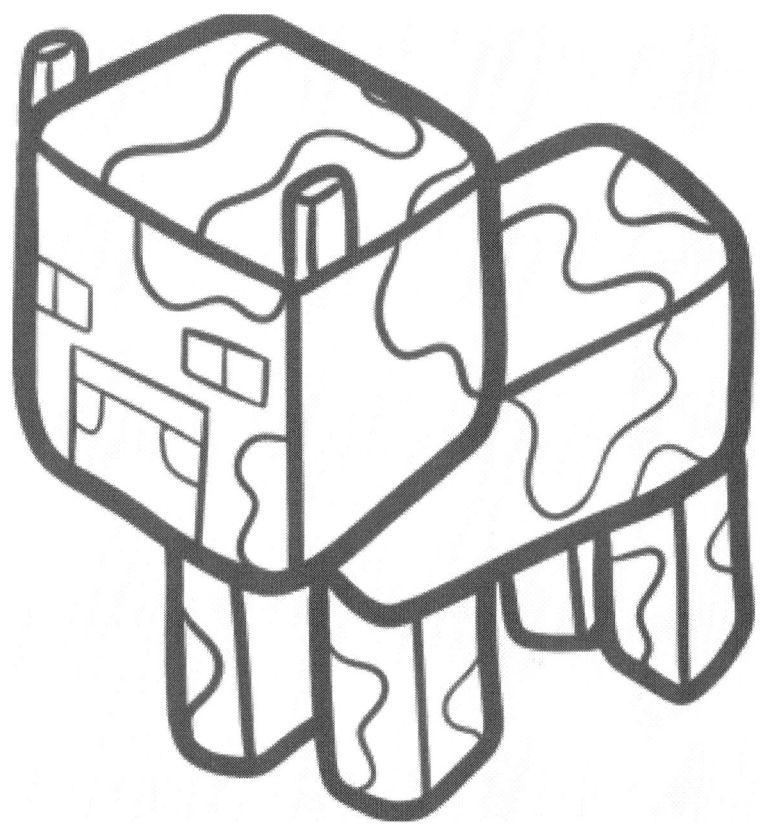

Now, you'll start drawing out the
complete pattern throughout the whole
body and face of your cow.
Congratulations, you're drawing is
now done!

Are You An Ultimate Stampy Fan?

If you are an ultimate Stampy fan, check out some of our best selling Stampy story books now available at *Amazon.com*!

The Adventures Of Stampy Cat (Parts 1-4)

"Bought it for my son and he loves it and Stampy."

"This book is very funny and made me laugh. Best book ever written. Especially because it's about Stampy Cat. Lol"

"Great book! I recommend this book to anyone who likes minecraft or stamps cat .try it on prime."

"I think this is a good book for me and all of the other stampy fans."

The Adventures Of Stampy Cat (Part 1)
The Adventures Of Stampy Cat (Part 2)
The Adventures Of Stampy Cat (Part 3)
The Adventures Of Stampy Cat (Part 4)

Stampy Cat Adventures: A Love Story

"I love how even though she got smacked with a stick she still knew that he was the one. Love!"

"OMG THIS BOOK IS AWESOME IF YOU ARE A STAMPY FAN YOU WILL GO NUTS WHEN YOU READ THIS!!!!!!!!
0"

Stampy Cat Adventures: The Big Friendship

Stampy Cat Adventures: StampyLongHead Meets His Nemesis

41300932R00033

Made in the USA
Middletown, DE
09 March 2017